Winter Games

Written by Roger Paré
with Bertrand Gauthier
and illustrated by Roger Paré

English adaptation by David Homel

Annick Press Ltd.
Toronto • New York

Annick Press Ltd.
All rights reserved. No part of this work covered by the copyrights
hereon may be reproduced or used in any form or by any means
– graphic, electronic or mechanical – without the prior written
permission of the publisher.

Annick Press gratefully acknowledges the support of the Canada
Council and the Ontario Arts Council.

Canadian Cataloguing in Publication Data
   Paré, Rober, 1929-
      (Plaisirs d'hiver. English)
      Winter games

   Tranlsation of: Plaisirs d'hiver.
   ISBN 1-55037-187-8 (bound).—ISBN 1-55037-184-3 (pbk.)

   I. Gauthier, Bertrand, 1945- II. Title.
   III. Title: Plaisirs d'hiver.   English

   PS8581.A697P52513   1991   jC843'.54
   PZ7.P375Wi   1991   C91-093461-4

The art in this book was rendered in water colour.
The text has been set in Bookman Light by Attic Typesetting.

Distributed in Canada by:
Firefly Books Ltd.
250 Sparks Ave.
Willowdale, ON M2H 2S4

Published in the USA by Annick Press (U.S.) Ltd.
Distributed in the U.S.A. by:
Firefly Books Ltd.
P.O. Box 1325
Ellicott Station
Buffalo, NY 14205

⊂⊃ Printed on acid-free paper.

Printed and bound in Canada by
D.W. Friesen & Sons, Altona, Manitoba.

For Dominik

We're going for a sleigh ride,
Won't you come along?
We'll glide through the snowdrifts
And sing a winter song.

First we'll visit Grandma
And have some cakes and tea,
And warm up by the fire
As cozy as can be.

Then the monkeys and the mice
Will have a snowball fight.
You hide in the igloo
And I'll stay out of sight.

Now when you see a squirrel
Busy knitting every day,
You know that Old Man Winter
Is really here to stay.

I'm sure that those two cats
Are both really wishing
They'd worn their woolen mitts
To go ice-fishing.

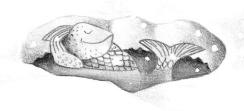

Did you see that snowy owl
In his downy, feathered suit?
Skiing through the woods,
With a squirrel, what a hoot!

Now follow close behind
And all hold on tight!
We're zipping down this hill
Faster than a kite!

When we ride on top
Of the elephant bus,
No one in these woods
Can catch up with us.

We're just in time
To see the bears-on-ice.
Here come the musicians,
A pair of skating mice.

But the best winter game
On a cold and snowy day
Is to stretch out by the fire
And giggle, laugh and play.

Other Annick Press books by Roger Paré:

A FRIEND LIKE YOU
SUMMER DAYS
CIRCUS DAYS
PLAY TIME